Parts of the (Church) Body

Written by Amanda Strater

Illustrated by Lauren Leibold

Illustrated by Lauren Leibold

WestBow Press books may be ordered through booksellers or by contacting:

WestBow Press
A Division of Thomas Nelson & Zondervan
1663 Liberty Drive
Bloomington, IN 47403
www.westbowpress.com
1 (866) 928-1240

ISBN: 978-1-9736-3756-1 (sc)
ISBN: 978-1-9736-3757-8 (e)

Library of Congress Control Number: 2018909951

Print information available on the last page.

WestBow Press rev. date: 8/28/2018

WESTBOW
PRESS®
A DIVISION OF THOMAS NELSON
& ZONDERVAN

Parts of
the (Church) Body

Marcus uses his fingers to play worship songs on the piano.

Can you move your fingers like you are playing the piano, too?

Jeff stands on his legs as he greets people coming into church.

Can you stand on your legs like a church greeter, too?

Presley rocks a baby in her arms as she helps in the Sunday school nursery.

Can you rock your arms like you are holding a baby, too?

Eric uses his ears to listen to the speaker volume as he adjusts the sound board for the church service.

Can you use your ears to listen, too?

Eve uses her eyes to read the Bible passages the pastor mentions during the sermon.

Can you move your eyes across the page, too?

Jenny lets her friend
lean on her shoulder and
comforts her.

Can you lend your shoulder
to a friend, too?

Fallon uses her tongue to taste refreshments some churchgoers brought to share.

Can you pretend to lick yummy food, too?

Michael bends his elbow as he vacuums the sanctuary after the church service is over.

Can you bend your elbow like you are vacuuming, too?

Roxanne kneels on her knees as she joins the prayer team to pray for others' needs.

Can you kneel on your knees and pray, too?

Wren uses her mouth to tell people about Jesus and the Bible.

Can you move your mouth like you are sharing the Gospel, too?

In the bible we learn that just as the body has many parts, so does Jesus' church. All your body parts serve important purposes, and everyone in church has an important purpose, too!

1 Corinthians 12:12 (NIV)

to each one, just as he
determines.   Just as a
body, though one, has
many parts, but all its
many parts form one
body, so it is with
Christ. For as we we
baptized

Jews or G
free

Even if you think you are small in size,
you are still essential. For example, ears
are small, but we need them to hear.

A child may be small, but a child can still do important things like pray and tell others about Jesus. How would you like to serve at church?

Thank you, Jesus, for all of our helpful body parts—big and small! And, thank you for the opportunity to be a part of your church and serve others.

CPSIA information can be obtained
at www.ICGtesting.com
Printed in the USA
BVHW02s1127150918
527587BV00007B/22/P